For all the Hen-dersons

First published 1996 by Walker Books Ltd
87 Vauxhall Walk, London SE11 5HJ

This edition produced 1999 for
The Book People Ltd, Hall Wood Avenue
Haydock, St Helens WA11 9UL

Printed in Hong Kong

ISBN 0-7445-3993-5

Dotty
the Hen

Kathy Henderson

TED SMART

Dotty the hen was pecking around in the dirt
when she found something.
"Look! Look!" she clucked.
"It's a worm, it's a worm!"

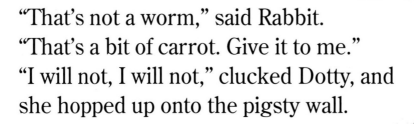

"That's not a worm," said Rabbit.
"That's a bit of carrot. Give it to me."
"I will not, I will not," clucked Dotty, and
she hopped up onto the pigsty wall.

Big Pig looked up.
"What have you got there?"
she grunted.
"It's a worm," said Dotty.
"That's not a worm," said Big Pig.
"That's a piece of spaghetti. Give it to me."

"I will not,
I will not,"
clucked Dotty,
and she ran
into the field.

"What have you got there?"
neighed Horse.
"It's a worm," clucked Dotty.
"That's not a worm," said Horse.
"That's a piece of grass. Give it
to me."
"I will not, I will not,"
clucked Dotty, and she
ran into the yard.

"What have you got there?" mooed the cows.
"It's a worm," clucked Dotty.
"That's not a worm," said the cows. "That's a
wisp of hay. Give it to us."

"I will not, I will not,"
clucked Dotty, and
she ran into the barn.

The kittens chased after her.
"What have you got there?" they mewed.
"It's a worm," said Dotty.
"That's not a worm," squeaked the
kittens. "That's a toy.
Give it to us."

"I will not, I will not, *I will not!*"
squawked Dotty.

And she ran out of the door and twice round the duckpond and all the way back to where she had started.

Just then the farmer's boy came
out to feed the chickens.
"Come and see what I've got
here," he called, pouring
chicken feed into their dish.
"Supper, supper,
supper."

Dotty the hen
dropped her
worm and
dived for
the food.

The farmer's boy bent down. "Oh, look," he said, picking up Dotty's worm. "I've been searching everywhere for this. It's my lost shoelace!"